DRAGONS

IRON

SOUP

FIREFLIES

TOO HOT

For my mom and dad,
who always made everything
just right.

Goldilocks and the Three Knocks
Copyright © 2022 by Gregory Arthur Barrington
All rights reserved. Manufactured in Italy.
No part of this book may be used or reproduced in any manner whatsoever
without written permission except in the case of brief quotations embodied
in critical articles and reviews. For information address HarperCollins
Children's Books, a division of HarperCollins Publishers,
195 Broadway, New York, NY 10007.
www.harpercollinschildrens.com

Library of Congress Control Number: 2021949598
ISBN 978-0-06-289137-2

The artist used pencil sketches scanned and painted in Adobe Photoshop,
with additional texturing applied with a scanned collage of handpicked
and dried maple leaves from his front yard to create
the digital illustrations for this book.
22 23 24 25 26   RTLO   10 9 8 7 6 5 4 3 2 1

First Edition

Goldilocks
and the Three Knocks

GREGORY BARRINGTON

Because I am Goldilocks.

Now, it's true. I did eat the bear's porridge.

Empty

Full

Sort of Full

I did break a chair . . . accidentally.

Oops

And, yes, I even took a teeny, tiny nap in a bed.

ZZZZZ

But that's not the WHOLE story.

You see, my story doesn't begin when *I* visit the three bears but when *they* visited me.

Once upon a time, one autumn day,
I moved into my new
home in the forest.

It had a just-right bed,

a just-right chair,

and a just-right kitchen, where I prepared low-carb, high-fiber meals that kept me feeling just right.

One day, there were three knocks on my door.

A big knock.

A medium knock.

And a tiny little knock.

KNOCK!

Knock!

Knock!

Now, let me tell you, if you live in the woods and you hear three peculiar knocks,

DO NOT OPEN THE DOOR!

But, of course, I did.

Standing at my door was a papa bear,

a mama bear,

a baby bear,

and a pie.

I'm not sure which one didn't knock.

"Hello, three strange uninvited bears with a pie. What could I possibly do for you?"

“TOO HOT! DON’T EAT!”

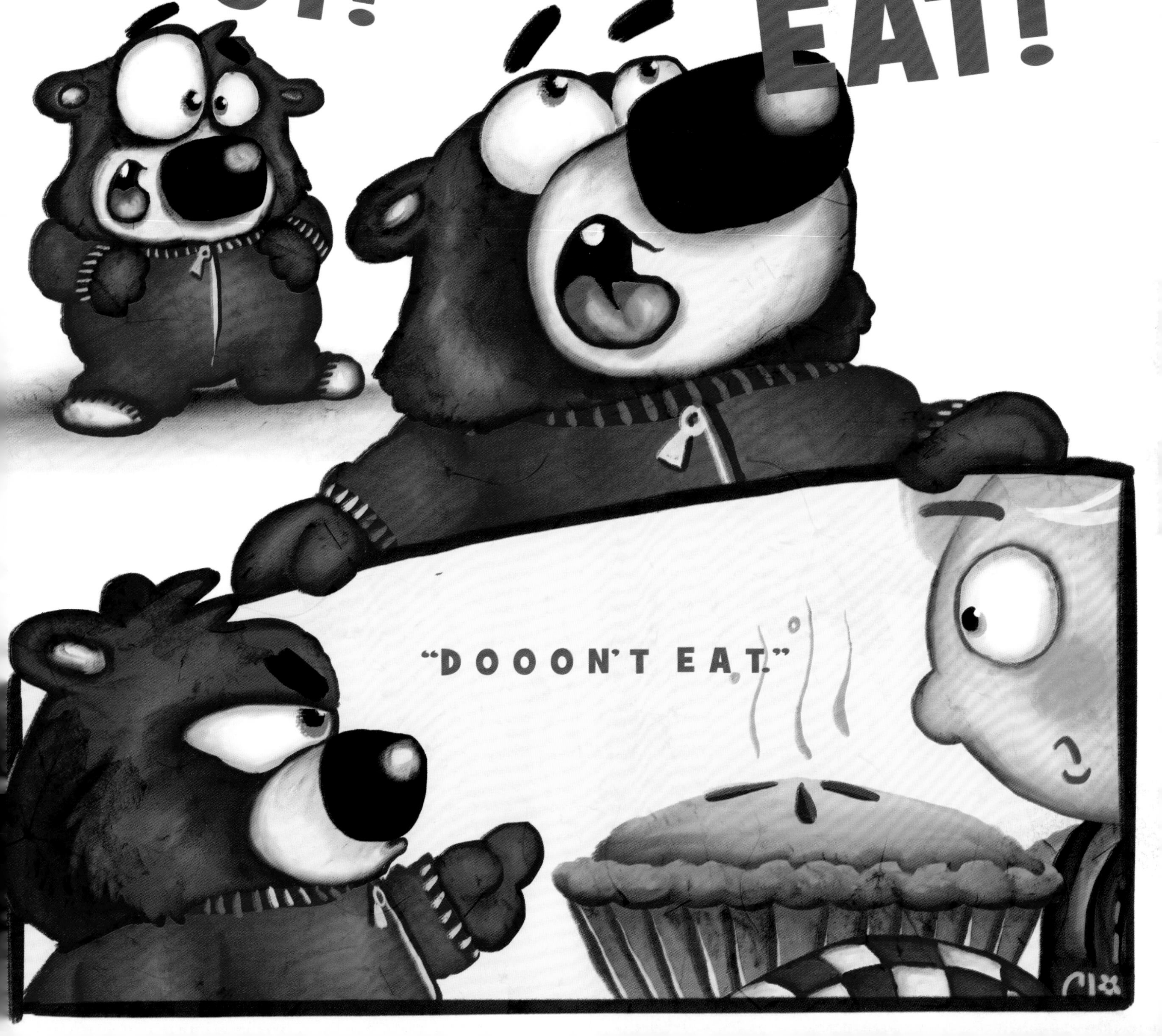

"No problem. We'll let the pie cool in the kitchen. Have a seat in my parlor and I'll bring us some just-right tea to drink while we wait."

But, of course, I did.

And when I returned, the bears were not in the parlor waiting to fix my chair.

They were not in the kitchen checking on the pie.

And they were not outside cleaning leaves from the gutters, which would have been REALLY nice of them to do.

Instead, they were taking a nap IN MY BED!

But as not to be rude, I let them sleep. After all, they did bring a pie.

The bears napped through the night
. . . and the entire next day.

That's when I
realized these
bears were not
napping in my
bed. . . .

They were

HIBERNATING

IN MY BED!

And let me tell you, bears hibernate for . . .

A V E R Y L O N G . . .

TIME!

And just when I was finally used to having those three lumps of snoring fur in my house . . .

they woke up.

"Happy spring, sleepy heads. I saved you some pie!"

"TOO COLD.

TOO COLD.

DON'T EAT!"

"DOOON'T EAT."

and you can try Papa Bear's perfect porridge, which I'm sure you'll find—"

"JUST RIGHT.

JUST RIGHT!

LET'S GOOOOO."

This last part is REALLY, REALLY IMPORTANT. If you are ever in the unfortunate situation where a bear invites you to visit their summer home anytime,

DON'T DO IT!

But, of course, I did.

Once upon a time, there was a girl named Goldilocks. One day, while walking through the forest, she stumbled upon a house. Goldilocks saw the front door was open and looked inside.